W9-BTF-989

For Cheryl

No part of this publication may be reproduced, stored in a retrieval system,
or transmitted in any form or by any means, electronic, mechanical,
photocopying, recording, or otherwise, without written permission of the publisher.
For information regarding permission, write to Hyperion Books for Children, an
imprint of Disney Children's Book Group, LLC, 114 Fifth Avenue, New York, NY 10011.

ISBN 0-439-80012-9

Text and illustrations © 2004 by Mo Willems. All rights reserved.
Published by Scholastic Inc., 557 Broadway, New York, NY 10012, by arrangement with
Hyperion Books for Children, an imprint of Disney Children's Book Group, LLC.
SCHOLASTIC and associated logos are trademarks and/or registered trademarks of Scholastic Inc.

50 49 48 47 46 45 44   17 18/0

Printed in the U.S.A.   40

First Scholastic printing, October 2005

The Pigeon Finds a Hot Dog!

The Pigeon Finds a Hot Dog!

words and pictures by mo willems

SCHOLASTIC INC.

New York   Toronto   London   Auckland   Sydney
Mexico City   New Delhi   Hong Kong   Buenos Aires

I have a
question.

What do they
taste like?

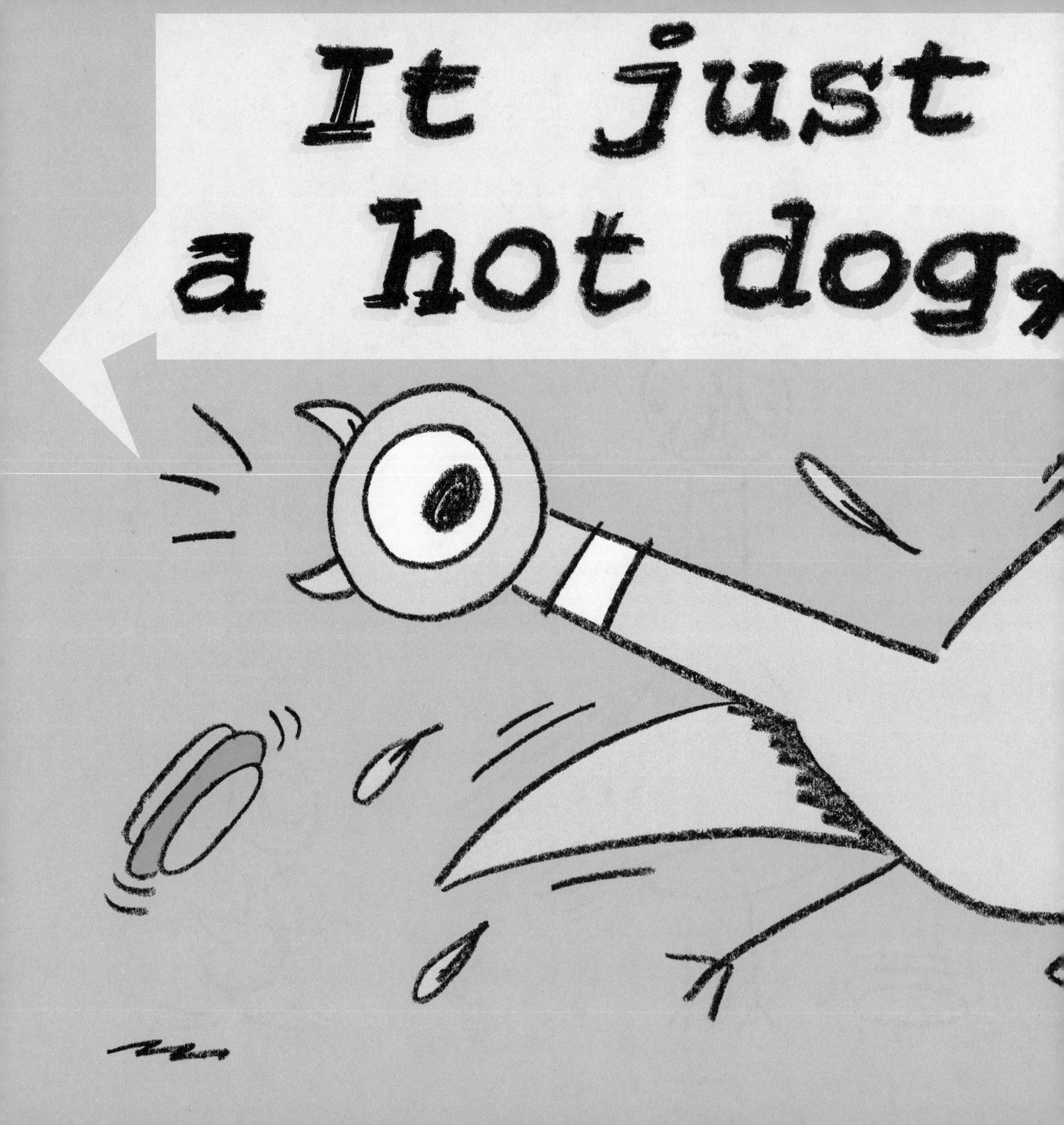
It just
a hot dog,

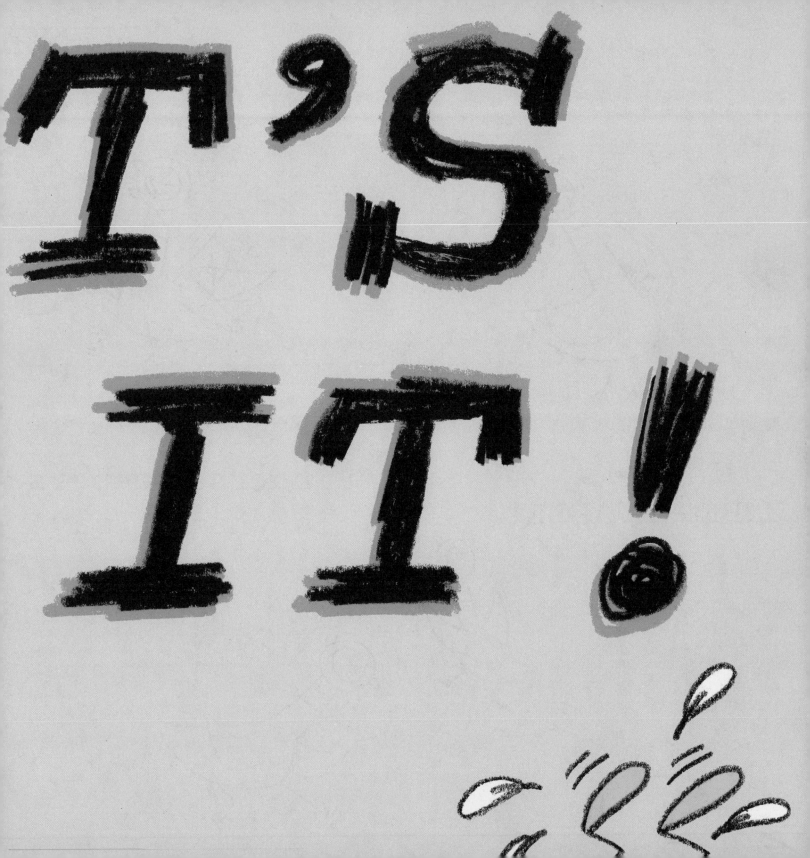

You know, you're pretty smart for a duckling.

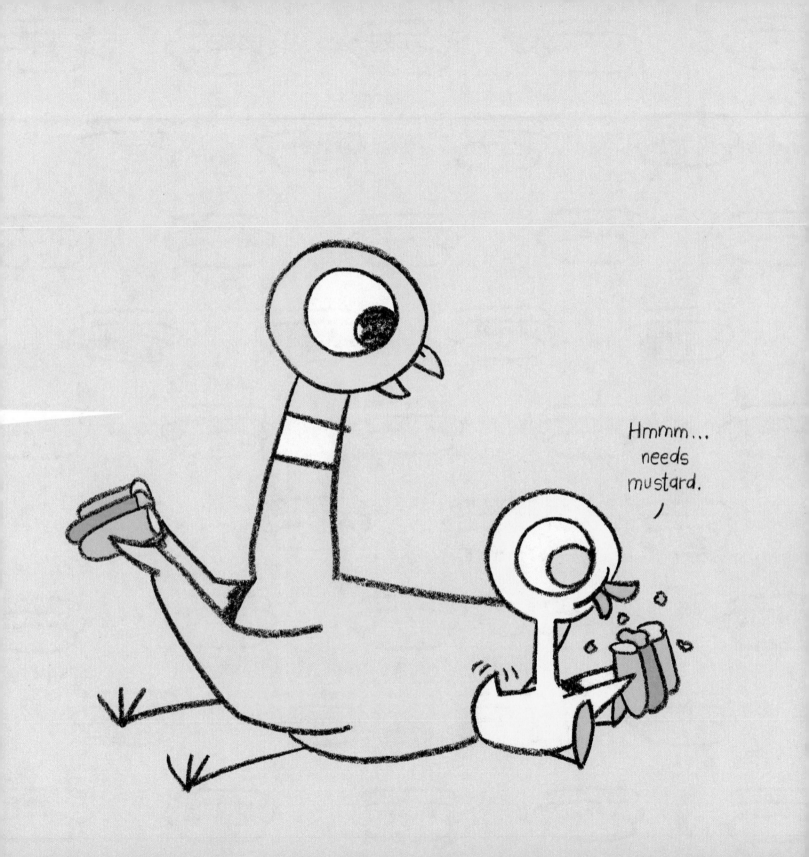